Aamna is a young Emirati author who enjoys sharing stories the reader can enjoy. *Hail* is her second short story, after *The Mysterious Shadow*. Yes, it is the beginning, and she herself is learning, but that is not a stop sign.

To everyone who thinks it's not possible.

Aamna Salem Bin
Hashel Al Tenaiji

# HAIL

AUSTIN MACAULEY PUBLISHERS™

LONDON • CAMBRIDGE • NEW YORK • SHARJAH

ISBN – 9789948779865 – (Paperback)
ISBN – 9789948779872 – (E-Book)

Application Number: MC-10-01-0539549
Age Classification: E

Printer Name: iPrint Global Ltd
Printer Address: Witchford, England

First Published 2023
AUSTIN MACAULEY PUBLISHERS FZE
Sharjah Publishing City
P.O Box [519201]
Sharjah, UAE
www.austinmacauley.ae
+971 655 95 202

*Hail* is a dream to be published. I can write paragraphs about this, but I'll just get straight to the point. There is no such thing as 'can't'; it's either will or won't. You do not know how much it means that you have this book in your hands. THANK YOU. I highly appreciate it, and I hope it comes to you as a reminder that you can do whatever you want. I know it sounds cliché, but it's really up to you.

# Prologue
## Latifa



As soon as the Adhan began, I stopped researching about horses (I have an unhealthy obsession), made sure I did my wudu, wore my prayer gown, and waited patiently for the Adhan to finish. Just when all of a sudden Baba called me.

"Latifa! Latifa!"

"Yes, Baba!"

I sprinted out, my prayer gown flying behind me.

"Call Khalifa, we're going to the masjid."

"Yes, Baba." And I treaded towards his room, bashing the door open. He had his back to me, playing some video games. Typical. I knew he wouldn't hear me, so I went and snatched his headphones off.

"Hey!" he blurted out, twisted his neck to face me, annoyed.

"Um… salah?" I said, both eyebrows raised, lips pressed.

"Oh, shoot!" He seized the headphones from my fingers aggressively and then, "Sorry, Shabab!"

I snorted, shaking my head with a grin. "Shabab?"

"Ad-dan!" Then he sent his headphones flying on his bed and set off fast, to do his wudu.

"Khalifa!" Baba shouted, clearly irritated.

"Sorry, Baba. I didn't hear you calling." He sprinted out of the bathroom; clothes soaked.

"Your clothes are wet," I demanded.

"It'll dry on the way." He smirked. "It's what? 45°C out?"

"43. Close." I patted him on the shoulder.

"Ya Allah, the Adhan will finish!" Baba complained.

And they set off. I shut the door behind them and made my way to pray.

# A Year Later
# KHALIFA

All Latifa is talking about are horses. Horses this, and horses that. She convinced Baba that I should ride instead of playing video games.

"Be present. Move. Win in real life."

And then she added, "And pray on time."

So now I'm taking lessons.

"Careful, Khalifa." That's what 13-year-old Latifa said to 13-year-old me before galloping on Toby for the very first time. Toby and I? We do not act jointly at all.

"I don't think I want to do this," I mumbled back.

"Just go!"

And so I did. I galloped and I was off and free, only when I loosened my grip on the bridle, lost my balance, and tumbled backwards on my back, as I and Toby forced the attachment of the wrong magnet, dissecting ourselves. I heard a crack as I slammed flat on the ground.

I opened my eyes, with them taking time to adjust. I tried sitting up, only when a sharp sting made its way up my spine, making my arms weak and brittle, sending me back to where I was.

*****

"Khalifa, careful." It was Latifa's voice. Rage flushed through me. These were her exact words I last remember hearing.

"Baba is speaking to doctors and he'll come back in—"

I decided not to—just not to—listen to what she has to say. But I couldn't, her voice was audible again. "—just that they didn't want me in the room with them, and they had nowhere to take me, so they just decided that—"

"Can you just—" and that's when the stinging pain shot up again, making me wince.

"Don't talk! Didn't I just tell you that, Khalifa?"

Turns out I thankfully did not break my back. I sprained it (did not know that such thing was possible, I thought spraining was an ankle thing) and it will take a month to recover. Great. One month of my summer break whilst accompanying the four walls of my bedroom, and Latifa's babbling mouth.

## Three Years Later

Four years later, and Latifa is screaming at my face, "That race, let it keep you going. You're not unsuccessful just because you didn't do it the first time, nor successful if you just do it once."

I just stared at her. Seems like she wasn't content with my response, she added, "Just because you fell, does not mean you don't ride. Just because someone burnt their cookies, does not mean they can't eat them. Just because a flight gets cancelled, does not mean you can't book another ticket. Just because—"

"These are literally nothing compared to falling off a horse," I replied, bored.

"Fine."

Just a couple of minutes later, I received an Email from the stables.

"What the…"

I clicked on the notification, with my phone detecting my thumb.

Just then, Latifa entered and said, "You're going. Baba paid."

# Chapter 1

## Khalifa

Summer afternoon, and the bus just pulled up in front of our villa to drop me from practice. It's 3:32 pm, and the road is steaming from the sun's heat. I was hopping off, managed to thank the driver, and put my hands on the metal bar to assist me, and for a second they were glued on. I went in through the huge, black gate, with the bus's loud engine slowly drifting away. I shut the gate and turned, with the interlock ground expanding before me. I walked, clothes pasted to my back, neck dribbling. Something was odd about our yard, until I noticed a new palm tree that had been planted. Baba has a devotion for trees, especially palm trees. It's a mother, the palm tree. Outside beside our main door was a huge cage with Barq, our falcon, in it. Latifa loves Barq so much, she's the main caretaker of him. I pushed the front door open dramatically, and saw my father watching the news as usual. Since I was fighting my dizziness, Baba beat me to it. "Assalamu alaikum!"

"Wa alaikum assalam." I went to plant a kiss on the apex of his bald, shining head.

"How was it? Riding?"

"I had fun, I'm feeling good—not now, I meant during practice."

"Mashallah! That's good to hear!"

"Yeah." I smiled.

My head is light, for a second I thought that it would fall off. I immediately back-flopped myself on the living room couch, suddenly feeling the cool air conditioner blowing around me. I sighed in relief.

When I started feeling a little bit better, I asked Baba, "What did you have for lunch?"

"Chicken saloona."

"Nice! Sad I wasn't here."

"There is some leftover—if you want some."

"No, it's okay, I already—"

"Shhh, let me listen to this," he said, lifting his palm up towards me. He then bent forward and squinted at the screen.

I looked at the TV screen, and it said 'BREAKING NEWS'. It filled the screen and was bright red. I have no interest whatsoever, so I plucked myself off the couch to take a shower so that I could get ready for prayer.

"Baba, I'm off to take a show—" I spoke, stopping myself, remembering that my voice isn't what's wanted to be heard at the moment. However, Baba was so engrossed that I don't think he picked up what I was saying. I began towards the hallway, heading towards my room.

## Latifa

Our house isn't huge, nor small. It's pretty decent. Throughout the same hallway where my room is, my brother's room, Khalifa, is facing mine. I wish we weren't facing each other, because when he plays with his PlayStation, he thinks that we're in a zoo. Anyways, Baba's room is down the hall, because he worries about us being down a hallway at night, which is pretty thoughtful. We have two kitchens in our house; one indoors, more like a kitchen-sized pantry with a stove and everything on the other hallway across from ours and straight ahead from the living, and another one outdoors, which is much bigger. It's mainly because of the smell. Since we have rice pretty much every day for lunch, we don't want our house to smell like fried onion, fish, chicken, spices, or whatever it is. We also have a majlis—two of them. Yes, you guessed it, one inside and one outside too. The one inside is less formal. The one outside is when there are 'special' people coming, or if it's Eid and Baba invited the fam for lunch. Across from our pantry-kitchen, we have a dining room.

I picked up my clothes from my white cupboard, and hurriedly paced myself to the bathroom to refresh.

# Chapter 2

## Khalifa

That's pretty much what happened every day, but today is the day before my race. I woke up to my blaring alarm at 6:30 am, to get ready for the bus at 7 am. I did the usual, wore my equestrian gear. 6:42 am. The bus should be here in a bit over fifteen minutes, enough time to eat breakfast. I walked towards the indoor kitchen, and on my way, I witnessed Baba sitting outside on the seating, one leg tucked under the other, with a newspaper. The grass under him looks beautifully green under him at this time of day, it caught my eye immediately. I opened the door and screamed out, "Good morning, Baba!"

He poked his head, startled, above the newspaper he was holding, and I could tell that he was chuckling from his shaking belly.

"Good morning, Khalifa!"

"A newspaper, I see?" I asked.

"Yeah, I saw it hanging on the gates' knob, thought I'd check it out."

"Nice, nice. Away from screens." I nodded teasingly.

"Yeah, a break, I suppose."

Ever since I started riding again, I realized the beauty of being present—and winning in real life. But that is something I'm going to find out today.

I stood in silence for a moment, admiring the clear sky, and the not-so-blinding sun that was radiating some warmth. It's cooler in the morning, 28 degrees. Not really cool. But still cool.

"You had breakfast?" Baba asked, folding the newspaper and placing it on the table in front of him.

"No, not yet. Thought I'd stop to see you first." I grinned.

"How lovely of you. Go fill up that empty stomach, I can hear it growling from here!" He chuckled again, this time, I could hear it.

I laughed and went into the dining room, as baba unfolded the newspaper and carried on skimming again. In the dining room, there was regag bread and karak milk in a thermos. I grabbed a plate and mug, took out some bread, and poured myself some milk. I folded the regag bread, making it into a triangle with a semi-circle base, and dipped it it's tip into the milk. As I was eating, the milk began running from the bread down onto my wrists.

When I finished, I checked the digital clock that's on the shelf, accompanied with a picture of me, Baba, and Latifa on a boat. Baba was fishing, and me and Latifa were spending the day with him. 7:05 am. I missed the bus. I shoved the last bit of bread in my mouth, drinking some milk along with it to soften it. I swallowed hard and sprinted towards the door. I put my hand on the doorknob, and it felt sticky. From the milk. I ran towards the kitchen, parkouring through furniture and rinsed my hands madly—I almost forgot to switch off the tap. I then made my way to the living room door to go outside, fussing to hear the click of it, and Baba peaked his head over the newspaper he's still reading.

"Woah, woah, woah. What's the rush?"

"I think I missed the bus," I blurted, devastated.

"Um, but isn't it only 6:55? I mean you better be ready now, before it shows up."

"Wait, what?" I furrowed my eyebrows, and plucked my phone from my backpack. It indeed is 6:55, just turned 6:56.

"It's the dining rooms' clock isn't it?" Baba asked.

"Yeah." I laughed quietly, rubbing my temples in disbelief.

"Happens. I always say I'll get it fixed but I forget. It didn't really matter to me until now."

Honking, not one, but two, came from outside.

"The bus is outside," we both called out at the same time.

I skipped down the stairs and went to kiss Baba on his head.

"Take care of yourself, Khalifa."

"Inshallah, Baba."

And I went towards the gate, to catch the bus before it leaves me behind.

# Chapter 3

## Khalifa

We arrived and I immediately entered the stable to see Copper, my horse. There were a bunch of boys reuniting with their horses.

"Copper!" I walked towards him and placed my palm in between his eyes and nostrils, feeling the heat escaping.

Copper is a chestnut brown Thoroughbred. I've been riding him for a while, and he's the best horse I've ever ridden—well, the only one unless you count Toby.

I placed the saddle on him, and hopped on. And we made our way to practice.

When I practice, I pretty much do whatever I want. So it is on my hands to win the race, and the pressure is heavy. Winning this race means I'll get to go and race abroad.

**********

"We did it!"

I was leading Copper back to the stable after practicing, and it's 2:45 pm. The heat is blazing through me, needles poking my skin. I'm just glad that the race will be tomorrow evening. Right when the sun is on its way to start a new day somewhere else.

I won't full-on practice tomorrow. I want to get enough sleep and let Copper recharge.

"I'll see you tomorrow," I said, connecting my eyes to his glinting ones, smiled, and then nodded lightly, making my way out to catch the bus ride back home.

# Chapter 4

## Khalifa

I'm back home, and as I walk in through the gate, I could feel my hair drenched with sweat. There it is, the dizziness again. It's like I'm in a dark cave with hundreds of heaters pointed directly at me. I stop in my tracks, in the middle of the yard, waiting for my dizziness to wear off.

"Khalifa?"

Baba.

"Yes, Baba!" I shouted back, and immediately resumed walking even though I did not gain my full sight back.

"You okay?" He asked.

"Yeah."

Sight is back. Baba is standing by the door.

I trod up the couple of stairs, and just as I was about to say my salam, he put both of his hands on my shoulders. "You were dizzy, right?"

I looked him directly in the eye. Then I looked back down to my boots.

"Yeah—but trust me, I'm okay!"

"Careful, Khalifa."

I've dealt with dizziness a lot here. It's hot. My nose even blee—

And there it is, I feel it. I cup my nose and Baba knows what that means.

**********

It's 7:22 pm, and I just got out of my room.

Baba was sitting on the couch, flipping through TV channels.

Latifa suddenly came to mind. "Baba, where's Latifa?"

"She's had a rough day. Barq's sick. She's in her room with a vacant gut."

"Wait—Barq's sick?"

Baba nodded; lips flat.

Barq is our falcon, and Latifa is so attached to him.

# Chapter 5


# Latifa


I am in my room, sitting on the edge of my bed, in the dark with only my bathroom lights illuminating a bit of my surroundings. I didn't bother to switch on my rooms' lights. Barq is flooding my brain, and it hurts.

There are muffled voices coming from the other side of the door, but then:

**KNOCK KNOCK**

"Latifa?" It's Khalifa. He never knocks.

"Yeah?" I sniff, fighting back tears. When someone is around and I'm feeling down, it's just easier to cry.

The door squeaked eerily as he opened the door.

"You okay?" He asked. He sounds genuinely concerned; I'm impressed.

"Yeah," I lied.

Khalifa began walking slowly towards me as if trying not to catch the attention of his predator. It's dead silent, I could hear his feet brushing the rug underneath.

I could tell that he was hesitant, but then he plopped himself on my bed beside me, making me bounce a little.

After a couple of silent minutes, Khalifa announced abruptly, "Baba wants to take us out for dinner. Get ready."

He picked himself up and made his way out. He then came back in and switched on the lights.

I smiled, sniffing and shaking my head, threw my Abaya and Wigaya on, and headed out.

I walked down the hall, and saw Baba already in his Kandura and Ghutra. He was standing in front of the mirror, fixing and adjusting his Agal. Seconds later Khalifa stepped out, wearing a Kandura, identical to Baba's.

Baba turned around and scanned us, smiling.

"Feeling better?" Baba asked me.

"Yeah," I replied, nodding with a small smile.

# Chapter 6

## Latifa

We got into Baba's Lexus: me on the passenger's seat, and Khalifa in the middle back.

Baba shoved in the car key, twisted it, and the engine began whirring, sending us all to vibrate in the car. Seconds later, we're off.

We were all silent, only when Khalifa did the honors of breaking the silence. "So where are we eating?"

"The one and only," he said, eyeing me from the side.

I grinned from ear to ear. I am starving. The last thing I ate was breakfast.

It was just as if Baba could read my mind, because he suddenly began, "Latifa, you should've eaten something."

I pressed my lips together.

"Yes, Baba." It startled me to hear my own voice.

"Wait, you didn't have lunch?" Khalifa jerked in.

I looked at Khalifa in the rear-view mirror and shook my head.

**********

The waiter came into our booth to get our orders.

"One shrimp biryani, and two Hamour biryanis."

"Any drinks?" The waiter asked.

We all shook our heads, with Baba adding, "No, thanks."

We are not the type of people that order drinks for some reason. We just go with water. Oh, and by the way, the shrimp is mine.

They brought in the freshly baked bread that had smoke diffusing from it, along with the variety of appetizers.

I dipped a piece of bread in the Hummus, chewed, swallowed, then ripped off another one, repeating the process.

Khalifa's arm barged in, extending in front of me. He grabbed the huge water bottle, pouring himself a glass of water—only when it spilled.

"Bismillah!" Baba exclaimed, grabbing some tissues.

"Whoops, that was not supposed to happen." Khalifa stood still, embarrassed.

"It's okay, Khalifa." I smiled, helping Baba with the tissues. "Just know, you can't predict the future, but that doesn't mean the worst is standing in line."

Khalifa eased up a bit, took the tissues from Baba's hands, then paused, when he heard that second part.

"What's that supposed to mean?"

"Why did you spill the water?"

"The bottle was huge."

"And you poured with two hands?"

"One."

"Don't go hard on yourself, stay reasonable."

"What?"

"When you're in bed tonight, it'll click."

And it's true. Because that night, he came into my room and woke me up.

"You mean the race, right?"

"What?" I sounded groggy and disgusting.

"When you're in bed, it'll click."

He made his way out and shut the door quietly.

# Chapter 7

## Khalifa

I woke up the next day, drowsy, yet still managed to collect myself and get out of bed. It took me a while to comprehend why I looked like I slept in a cave. When I looked at the clock, it was 10:47 am. This is not normal. I am so used to having people bash into my room randomly (Latifa), but today no one even bothered to knock… Or maybe it's me who didn't hear, but that's not the point.

I missed practice!

Oh.

Race. Race!

I got up, and did the morning usuals, and headed out to the living room.

Baba was watching the news; habitual.

"Big day," he remarked.

"Big day," I approved. "Good morning—by the way," I added hastily.

"Good morning," he chuckled. "Go have breakfast."

"Yes, Baba. Where is Latifa?" I asked.

"Probably asleep."

"You're so chill about it lately."

"About what?"

"Us sleeping in."

"As long as you wake up to pray, then I don't have a problem. It's summer, and I was a kid once. It's not that you'll do anything beneficial if you wake up."

"Yeah, well, okay." I smiled without showing the pearly whites.

"And Barq, he's well."

"Really?"

"I'll let her know when she wakes up," he smiled.

Breakfast today is chabab bread. I love chabab bread. It's like a pancake. You can eat it with honey, sugar, cheese, or whatever you want, really. I like it with honey the most. So I grabbed the honey glass bottle, unscrewed the lid, and poured in some on my plate. I then grabbed some bread and began munching, filling up my stomach. All that was on my mind was the race. It was becoming overwhelming only when thankfully, Latifa joined me at the dining table.

"Morning," she said it as if insulting me.

"Morning," I replied. "What's wrong?"

"What?" She asked.

Latifa is always tempered in the morning.

"Want some bread?" I asked, at the same time as she said, "Give me some bread."

I think Baba forgot to tell her about Barq.

"Barq is all good." I looked at her, smiling.

Latifa stared at me for precisely three seconds, a smile growing on her face. She then ran out of the dining room.

# Chapter 8

## Khalifa

The moment has come. Dad drove me to where the race will be held, along with Latifa. There are no buses when there's a race.

"Don't forget to—"

"Yes, Khalifa, for the five hundredth time, I will not forget to record you."

"Khalifa, relax yourself," Baba chuckled softly. "I know you feel a bit agitated, but that's not going to do you any good, will it?"

I nodded, staring at my jet-black polished boots.

We pulled up, and Baba had to drop me first so that I can get Copper ready.

"We'll wait here until they let us viewers in."

"Yes, Baba."

Baba seemed to be able to tell that I was a bit rigid.

"Don't forget to breathe," he reminded quietly.

"Yes, Baba." I smiled nervously.

I walked towards the gate. The security guard is already familiar with me, so he let me in without any questions.

I walked my way to the stables and found Copper.

"Hey, Copper," I spoke, walking towards him.

Copper nickered softly in return.

**********

RACE.

All the horses were lined up. Ten racers. I am nerve wrecked. The sun still hasn't set, but it's not very hot; more like warm.

"On your marks!"

A pause.

"Get set!"

Another pause.

"Go!"

All the horses on both my sides set off, and it took me a while to realize what was going on.

The guy on the speakers began shouting, "Go! Go! Go!"

I didn't know if it was directed at me, or if it was some cheering for the racers that already took off, whilst I was still hanging back, unnoticed.

"I will need you to dash, Copper," I spoke to him, and then I took off.

Everything happened so fast, that the horses in front of me still weren't a distance away.

*I had a chance.*

Copper transformed into a cheetah, sprinting so elegantly and smoothly. We were last—technically, but we forged ahead a racer, leaving them trailing behind.

One down.

I looked ahead of me, and I knew, and I knew that copper knew, because just seconds later, we beat two horses that were frictioning against each other.

Three down, six left. I could hear the faint sound of families and friends cheering.

The finish line is still distant. There were two horses in front of me that were beginning to slow down. I knew Copper was going to slack too at some point since he made a dash with all his energy and power at first. *No. Please, no.*

I bent a little bit forward, close to his pointy ear.

"Copper, please. Copper, I—"

And there it was. He felt, sensed; he knew. Out of nowhere, Copper whinnied, stood on his hind legs, and sprinted, as if his battery had been replaced. He bolted; threw the dart.

"Copper!" I whisper-shouted.

He neighed in reply; as if reassuring me.

I shut my eyes and let him do the job. I trust him, but I still had fear building up inside me.

"Victor!" I heard a guy complain behind me, scolding his horse. I opened my eyes; the world was bouncing around me. Only one left. One racer left. Its racer was far away.

This is going to be tough. Every practice. Becoming dizzy, bleeding my nose. I was not going to let this slip. Apology in advance to whoever it is that thinks they won.

I locked eyes on the person bobbing in front of me.

"We got this copper."

Copper dashed, lighting fast.

I clenched my jaw, held on to the brittle tightly, and…

… I made it. I won.

I heard cheering behind me, only when Copper went up on his hind legs, and neighed loudly in victory. My grin was from ear to ear, I couldn't believe what just happened.

# Chapter 9

## Khalifa

"Khalifa!" I heard my sister shaking my shoulder violently. "Get up! We're going to be late!"

I opened my eyes with the bright white lights of my room flashing painfully through my pupils.

"Can you like, switch the lights off?" I spoke casually, but with grog in my voice.

"I said, get up!"

I looked at the digital clock on my nightstand, and I just groaned. It was 3:39 am.

"It's three thirty-ni—"

"Our flight is at eight!" she *yelled*, after rolling her eyes. She then shouted, "You know what?"

*What?* I thought, but didn't say it. I covered my chin with my blanket, squinting to look at her, brows stitched.

"I don't really care anymore, because it's not me competing, isn't it?" She scolded with dramatic hand gestures. She then proceeded towards the door, and slammed it with all her will, rattling the whole house.

No idea how she has all that energy at three in the morning.

I got up and stretched. I felt heavy, like the bed was some magnet that was attempting to pull me in. I nearly fell for the bait only when Latifa—quickly, yet gracefully—opened the door, and added, "And you also have to get ready for prayer." Then she slammed the door again, making me flinch.

## Latifa

Absolutely ridiculous.

# Chapter 10

## Khalifa

"—prepare for landing," is the only thing I understood from the pilot's muffled speaking.

I was lying down—asleep—for most of the flight. Latifa was generous enough to keep me asleep whilst adjusting my seat to its default state, and by tightening my seat belt.

I opened my mouth to thank her, only when Latifa said, "How was your beauty sleep, princess?"

I could tell that she was teasing, and now I was glad that I didn't thank her.

**********

Pulling a small suitcase trailing behind me, Baba, Latifa, and I made our way out of the plane and in through the jet bridge. Latifa looked in pain with her huge tote bag on her shoulders.

"Give me that," I demanded.

"Thanks." She gave me the bag and rubbed her sore shoulder, making a face. She then smiled nervously, trying to appease me, I guess.

We then got a bit lost, trying to figure out where we could claim our suitcases, only when Baba paused mid-walk, eyebrows wrinkled, looking at his phone's screen.

"I have a lot of missed calls from the stables, Khalifa."

I came to a halt, followed by Latifa.

This could either be good, or bad.

"Baba, call back," Latifa said. My mouth was sealed shut; throat clogged.

"Hello?" Baba somewhat greeted. "Oh, okay… okay… okay… Yes."

Latifa and I exchanged glances; confused.

"What are we going to do about that?" That question made my stomach whir. "All right, thank you."

Baba pulled his phone down from his ear, inhaled fast, sucking in the whole airport.

Latifa and I stared expectantly, waiting for something to be pronounced.

"Copper is dead."

# Chapter 11

## Latifa

Two days later, and Khalifa's still devastated. We just prayed Al-Duhr prayer, and now we're sitting in our hotel room. It's a bit hard because of the time difference and not hearing an Adhan, but we managed to fathom. Khalifa was lying in bed, scrolling mindlessly through his phone. His coping mechanism, I suppose. I was sitting on a comfy lounge chair, and Baba was watching the news. I don't know if it's the news that's chasing Baba, or the other way around, but every single day, Baba has to watch it. Even on the plane.

I was starting to become hungry; my stomach was screaming audibly. The day here is way longer than back home.

"Food? Anyone?"

"I'm not hungry." That's what Khalifa has been saying since we got here, even though he always ends up eating whatever we order him.

"Let's eat on the balcony," Baba suggested. He heard me: let history record.

"Oh yes!" I replied enthusiastically.

The weather here is much cooler, so the balcony will be a different change.

I picked myself from the lounge chair briefly, and stretched my arm towards Khalifa's nightstand. I plucked the menu from its holder and began flipping through. I began reciting, "Pasta, soup, rice—"

Then Baba interrupted, "What rice options do they have?"

"Chicken, shrimp, fish—"

"What kind of fish?"

"It's not mentioned; it just says 'fish'."

"All right, I'll just go for the chicken."

"Inshallah, Baba. I want pasta."

"Great! And Khalifa?"

We both looked at him, question in our eyes.

"I want pasta, too." He sat up and smiled.

I looked at Baba, puzzled.

"Pink sauce," he added. "Can't decide whether I would like red or white sauce."

I checked if that was an option, and it was. So I just nodded and smiled back.

---

Just managed to settle myself on the edge of the bed Khalifa was lying on to watch TV with Baba (not that I was interested, it was just that I had nothing to do), only when a low knock was sounded at the door.

"The food," Baba and Khalifa mumbled at the same time.

No idea why both of them had to point that out.

Khalifa went to fetch the door like usual, however, this time, he actually looked normal. The switch has been flipped.

"Thank you," I heard him say, whilst shutting the door, clicking it carefully.

He came in, pushing the rattling serving tray.

I got up and helped him push it over the carpet.

I set the food out on the balcony table and called them out to eat.

I handed Baba his rice, gave Khalifa his pasta dish, and placed my plate in front of me.

"Bismillah," Baba said, followed by Khalifa and me. Baba took no notice of his utensils, hitting with the five. Khalifa stabbed his cooked grains with a fork, with me doing the same too.

Moments later, Baba got up. "Alhamdulillah."

I gathered courage to ask Khalifa before he got up too.

"What was that about?"

"What was what about?"

"The sudden—"

"Mama."

I was silent.

He smiled a tiny, sad smile.

"Alhamdulillah," he said, and got up.

I stayed there looking out at the view. Green was filling my sight. It was all so beautiful. A bird landed on the rail, tilting its head and fidgeting about. I looked at it, and my stare must've been intimidating, because as soon as my pupils placed themselves on the bird, it fled away.

# Chapter 12


## Latifa

"This evening, we're going to go to an ancient, antique palace," Papa declared as if he just won a Nobel prize.

"Um, can't we go somewhere else?" Khalifa asked, looking genuinely bored.

"Trust me, you'll have fun."

Forced into the car Baba rented, I and Khalifa slept through the whole journey.

"Wake up, you two! We're here!" Baba called out from the front seat. Baba seems so thrilled about this palace, it was concerning. I fixed my headscarf and got out of the car.

We walked across the entrance hall with a bunch of other tourists, crossing the golden chandelier above us, and went up the colossal curved, carpeted stairs.

"This is her highness' room," the docent said.

We looked into the room with some "*ooooh*s" and "*aaaaahs.*"

The docent then guided us to the next room. "And this is her daughters' room," he informed.

I could tell that Khalifa was trying to be polite, concealing a yawn, but it was still visible.

We carried on entering, gazing, then leaving many rooms until we made it to the exit. It was actually pretty interesting, so I did enjoy my time—a bit.

"Before you all go," the docent began, "I would like to thank you for taking a tour. Rate the tour five stars under my name, please."

"Finally," Khalifa exhaled. But when he heard the last bit he snorted.

He pulled his phone out and actually did rate him five stars. I patted him on the back, pleased. He ordered me to do the same thing, and I did.

We were on our way out when Khalifa saw a horse museum.

"Can I check the museum out?"

"Sure!" Baba said, flattered.

Baba gave Khalifa money so that he can cut himself a ticket.

"Call us when you're done."

"Inshallah, Baba. Latifa, want to join me?"

"No, I'm good. Go have some alone time."

He nodded, authentically contented, and turned away before it got too crowded.

"Let's stroll by the fountain and have a seat on one of the benches," Papa suggested.

"Yes, Papa," I replied obediently.

We passed a huge marble water fountain, lit up with bright white lights in this tranquil evening—that is in the midst of the whole huge ground; between the bronze entrance of the palace and the huge metal, silver gates of the whole palace yard—which was spraying water calmly, giving off this peaceful sound. We turned to the left side of the palace, which was covered with fresh grass. The beautiful, crisp smell of nature whiffed.

We made our way towards the benches parked on the edges of the grass, and sat.

I looked up at the soundless, dark sky, crowded with flickering, glimmering stars.

"What are you thinking, Latifa?" Papa asked, quietly; not wanting to ruin the peacefulness.

"I don't know, Baba." I shrugged.

Baba rubbed my back, and I added, "My mind is crammed. All my thoughts are confined, needing more space."

"I know what that feels like," Baba admitted.

"Yeah. It's just, you know. Khalifa."

This race was all he had on his mind, but now that Copper is gone, this trip is just pointless.

"Yes, but it's not like he's trying to forget." Baba looked at me. "He went to a *horse* museum."

We sat for a moment and then, "Baba?"

"Yes, darling."

"What are we going to do for the remainder of the days here, since—you know, there will be no, um, race?"

"I'll take you two to a campsite."

"Interesting." I sounded less interested than I actually was.

"Trust me, you'll enjoy it."

"As long as Khalifa is satisfied," I spoke, smiling.

# Chapter 13

## Khalifa

Today we're going to a campsite, but we're not going to stay for the night.

The weather was a bit contradictory; a summer afternoon, but a bit gloomy outside, which was quite odd. We all assumed that it was just passing clouds.

We got in the car, and since we were running low on gas, Baba stopped at a gas station. I stayed up with Latifa all night last night playing some video games. We both felt tired, so we winded down, falling silent, until we slept.

I suddenly woke up, groaned, then muttered, "Are we there yet?"

"Not, *yet*," Baba replied.

My expression fell blank.

"But we're nearly there," Baba added as if he could see me.

"Oh!" My expression switched back, and I smirked.

When we arrived, I woke Latifa up.

"Latifa, we arrived," I said, shaking her shoulder.

She woke up and stared at the window, zoned out.

Baba checked the weather forecast and said that it was not going to rain which left us all at ease, sighing sighs of relief.

Don't get me wrong, we love the rain, but not in the middle of a campsite. When we got out of the car, we walked across moist grass towards a forest. A huge unlit forest. There were some tents set in areas, far away from each other.

# Latifa

We had a long walk; my legs were smarting. They felt like needles were being pinched deep inside them. We then abruptly paused to scan the area, looking for a great spot to bring our tent to life.

We went closer to the area and examined it, and it turned out to be perfect. The only downside about it was that it was in the middle of nowhere, between ginormous trees, all indistinguishable to one another, with no figure to be seen. Nonetheless, Baba and Khalifa agreed to plant the tent in an area in which I was a bit indecisive. Baba noticed my stiffness and intensity, so he came towards me and reassured, "It's safe. Don't worry."

Baba began unzipping the fairly big bag that had the tent in it. He unfolded it with the help of Khalifa and I, and then laid it on the damp ground. Khalifa and I looked at each, puzzled about how on earth we were going to set that tent up.

Baba looked at us, grinning.

Baba and I began attempting to set the tent up, whilst Khalifa was asked to garner some wood so that we can light up a fire.

We tried several times, but we always ended up putting it up in the most erroneous ways.

Khalifa came just in time, struggling to carry the bag of wood.

The bag looked tremendously heavy, he looked that he could barely move his legs and his arms were limply trying to get hold of the bag like they're about to be plunged through the ground. He began staggering lopsided like a truck on the edge of a hill.

"Gold in disguise," Khalifa exclaimed breathlessly, looking at the wooden sticks stacked in the bag.

When Baba took notice of Khalifa, he darted to help him carry the bag. He took it away from him and positioned the bag on his arms pointing forward, with it leaning against his chest.

"It *is* heavy," Baba concurred whilst Khalifa nodded aggressively.

"You gathered more than enough, Khalifa." Baba chuckled.

Baba then put the bag on the ground, clapped his hands to get the dust off.

Khalifa saw that the tent was still flat.

"Still didn't set the tent up?"

"Nope," I admitted, even though it was obvious.

"It's okay," he reassured, "Three brains are always better than two, because you guys forgot this piece," he spoke, lifting up the most important piece from the bag.

We laughed hysterically at ourselves as if a joke had been told.

As we were setting up the tent, it was nearly evening. Baba set up the wood in a neat way, then he pulled out a match. He lit up the match and the fire spread, causing a very astonishing effect, captivating the eye. The fire just escalated around, making *all the birds of a feather flock together*.

Time passed as we were relaxing and admiring the peaceful nature. The sun was setting which created a gorgeous vibrant sky, colors from red, to orange, yellow, pink, and even a glimpse of purple.

"Time for some marshmallows!" Baba sounded as excited as we are.

We sat beside each other, by the warm, console fire, and stretched our arms to watch our marshmallows burn, slowly having its white color fade, turning into a cocoa brown color. It smelled incredibly tempting, literally asking to be eaten. And of course, I couldn't refuse Mr. Marshmallow's demand. I nodded and sent my hand on a mission to arrive right inside my mouth.

# Chapter 14

## Khalifa

The next day, we woke up early because Baba decided to take us to a park that's beside the woods. That sounded eerie.

"It's like a park but with giant trees. We'll have a picnic, and participate in activities like zip lining and—"

"Zip lining?" Me and Latifa shouted in unison.

"Keep your voices down! We have people on the other side of the wall!" Baba chuckled.

"Baba you do not have to carry on your list. Khalifa and I are going!" Latifa's smile filled her whole face.

That's not something you do every day, so I and Latifa were overflowing with excitement, interested and eager to see how that would go.

I could tell that Baba was trying to please us after the incident, which I really do appreciate.

"We'll grab snacks on the way."

"Yes, Baba."

We exited the hotel and walked towards our car. It was a sunny morning, but there was still a refreshing cold breeze.

"First we're going to buy something we can sit on."

And we did. But all the blankets there were obnoxiously huge and heavy. We left and went to another store. Same thing. So we ended up purchasing one, nevertheless.

Baba then stopped in front of a grocery store. "C'mon. Get whatever your heart desires," Baba generously offered.

"Thanks Baba!"

Pushing the door as we went in, a bell rang above us. The grocery was quite small, so we knew which aisle to go to. Latifa's weak spot is chocolate, so that's the aisle she went for. I am more of a crackers person.

"It's because I'm sweet, and you're always salty," Latifa would always deride.

I grabbed some cheddar crackers and barbeque flavored ones. My absolute favorite. Latifa grabbed a bunch of chocolate.

"Chill, Latifa, you won't find a golden ticket."

Baba bought an average laban and a chicken sandwich.

We were back in the car, and looking out the window, a blur of green bushes zoomed on either side of us. Latifa was staring out the window, waving to little kids in cars. Typical Latifa. She's always herself, whether she's pleased or vexed.

I looked at my phone's screen and it just turned 9:00 am. My phone suddenly began to chime ridiculously; even Baba and Latifa questioned.

I opened up my messaging app and saw that it was exploding with messages. One after the other. I was not in the mood to see whatever the pandemonium is about, and either way, we are supposed to have fun together: Baba, Latifa, and me. So I put my phone on 'Do Not Disturb', and gave it to Latifa so that she could secure it with her protected cross body handbag. She values that thing heavily.

**********

After going up a hill, we arrived. 9:41 am. Not bad, not bad.

"Woooooo! I can't wait!" Latifa squealed.

Papa laughed and I smiled.

Baba drove us in, we went through some security checks, then made our way to the parking lot. I was carsick and wanted to get out of the car so badly, and at last, I had the ability to do so. The parking lot had some tiny puddles of water jotted at random areas.

"Seems like it rained here, most likely last night," Baba let us know.

"I hope it rains sometime whilst we're here," I remarked.

"Yeah, it barely rains back home," Latifa added.

"Say Alhamdulillah either way," Baba said, unbuckling his seatbelt. "C'mon, let's go!"

Latifa grabbed the bag of snacks, and I the heavy blanket. Baba offered to take the blanket from me (I guess it was obvious that I was struggling), but I refused. I put the blanket above my shoulder and held it with both arms. This way—I realized—made carrying it easier.

We walked into the park and I was left astonished.

Latifa's eyes were literally bulging.

"Latifa, careful, your eyes will roll out," I teased.

She smiled sheepishly in return.

After walking for a while, Baba, behind me, told us to stop and lay the blanket, and so I did, only when I realized that Baba was helping me carry the blanket the whole time.

"Thanks, Baba." I smiled blushing.

"My pleasure." He nodded.

We sat on the blanket under the sun rays—we didn't even mind the sun: it wasn't blinding nor hot. Latifa began plucking the freshly cut grass, a habit of hers.

Baba admired nature, then exclaimed, "Subhan Allah!" His face was filled with glee. He looked younger, happier.

Latifa put the bag of snacks on the corner and ordered us to sit so that we could take a picture together.

"Let's recharge before zip lining, which I assume is what you want to do first."

"Indeed!"

## Latifa

Whilst we were eating, a row of yellow school buses made its way into the entrance, with a bunch of elementary students vacating the bus. They were lined up in single files, with a teacher in front of each line.

When they began walking, some children were craning their necks and gawking around which made me chuckle silently. The teachers began clapping their hands loudly together to get the attention of all the young children. They were saying something and gesturing, but they were a bit far that I couldn't make out what they were saying. But, out of nowhere, a butterfly showed up, distracting me, fluttering its thin, superfine, tiny white wings. It was peculiar yet prepossessing. I have never seen one before. It landed on the back of my hand, and I freaked out and recoiled. The butterfly in return let its wings guide its next destination, exquisitely.

We zip lined and biked. Khalifa rock climbed. Then we went to grab some lunch. They offered some in a canteen, which wasn't that bad at all. We sat down at the far corner of the canteen, facing each other with red, blushed faces after the exhaustion despite the excessive amount of fun physical activities we've been occupying ourselves with.

After lunch, we headed back to our blanket which was thankfully still there (we left it because it was heavy). Looking up at the sky, herds of dark concrete grey clouds began turning into charcoal.

"Looks like it's going to rain," Baba informed.

"Yeah, we better get—" I started, but then a movement caught my eye. I saw one of the elementary students—I could tell by the uniform—on a horse, being led by a woman giving him a walk. I got up abruptly, dusted my pants involuntarily, muttered, "One minute," then sprinted towards the woman.

"Excuse me," I said, breathing awkwardly, trying to get myself together.

She was young, a bit older than me, perhaps, and was wearing an equestrian set.

"Yes?" She spoke politely.

"The horse—" I breathed, "Where did you get—" I breathed another breath, "the horse from."

"This horse is mine. But there is a stable all the way there" – she pointed, across the playground – "if you're interested."

"Yes, thank you." I smiled, pleased. My pieces were just put together: breathing even. But they fell apart again, because I ran back towards Baba and Khalifa.

"Khalifa!" Latifa called out.

"Latifa!" I called back, absorbing the elation.

"Good news!"

"What's up?"

"There's a horse stable," she told me, grinning.

"Yeahhh…?"

"Which means, go find yourself a horse and race." Baba popped in.

"Really?" My eyes widened, nearly popping out of their sockets.

"Careful, your eyes might roll out—whatever," Latifa mimicked me.

I actually laughed.

# Chapter 15

## Khalifa

"What are you waiting for? Let's go!" Latifa grabbed my arm and yanked it.

I got up and began to follow her.

"I'll wait for you here!" Baba shouted.

"Yes, Baba!" I shouted back and put a wonky thumbs up with my free arm.

"The stable is across the playground," Latifa informed me.

"How is—"

"Just follow me!" she hissed.

*What's with your temper?* I wanted to ask, but I just shut up.

We kept fast-walking, until abruptly, Latifa shouted, "There!"

And indeed, it was there. An obnoxiously huge stable.

"Are you sure that we're allowed to—"

But Latifa already took-off, leaving me to trail behind.

"Sir," Latifa began to the security. "May we go in?"

"I'm afraid you can't."

Before we could protest, he said, "You are not a member."

"Well, then may I become a member," she spoke impatiently. I can tell she had the urge to roll her eyes.

"You can't just *become* a member."

"Hey! Hey, you two!" The three of us turned around, and we saw a man and a girl on horses, making their way towards us.

"What's going on?"

"Sir, these two want to come into the stables, but they are *not* members," the guard spoke.

"Nah man. It's all good." He then looked at the girl beside him and said, "Sierra, show the girl around, and I'll take the young man."

"Yes, Dad," Sierra replied.

The security guard looked evidently agitated.

"Sorry," I saw Latifa mouth.

But he just departed as if we smelled bad.

We entered the stables and wow. Just *wow*. It's huge, filled with dozens of horses. And I was able to catch on most breeds. Thoroughbred's, Appaloosa's, Belgian's, Gypsy's, and many more. The more I walked, the more horses I saw.

"So what brings you here?" The guy asked me.

"Umm, I like to ride," I uttered.

"Huh," he said, as if I showed him how to work out a complicated math problem.

"Which breed do you ride?" He asked, slowly.

"Thoroughbred," I answered.

"Nice."

We kept on walking.

"Other than thoroughbreds," he started, "which horse do you want to ride?"

"Arabian."

It is a dream for me to ride an Arabian. Ironic since I literally come from a place where I can easily find one. But I have—had—Copper, and it felt like betrayal to just abandon him from a different horse.

"Never raced?"

"Oh, I actually did. I got first." I smiled slightly. "But that was not an official race, just to determine if I could race here."

"Really? When's the race?"

"In two days, but, um…" I hesitated.

The man looked at me expectantly.

"My horse, Copper, died." That tasted disgusting.

"Oh… oh, I'm so sorry." I could see the bitter sadness in his eyes.

"Yeah, thanks, I guess."

He seemed genuine. Like he has lived with horses, which is true—based on what I can see.

"You know, I lost five horses in my life. And each loss is harder than the previous. They're not just horses, they feel, and they understand."

He nodded one fast nod and pressed his lips into a flat line. He rubbed my back, then said, "Follow me." And I did.

We walked, passing many horses, until I stopped in front of one that looked at me differently.

"An Arabian," I muttered under my breath.

Majestic, handsome, mystical. That's the Arabian. It's color obsidian, along with his silky mane and tail.

"You could tell," he spoke, seeming surprised.

"Yes, sir."

He chuckled. "You don't have to call me that. In fact, don't. Even Jason—the security guard. No idea why he calls me that."

I smiled. "Then what should I call you? Mister…?"

"Nah man. Call me Nathaniel."

I smiled and walked closer towards the horse. The horse looked at me, as if he's known me for years.

"What's his name?"

"This pal is still not named. Do the honors and give him one."

Nathaniel put his hands behind his back, and began walking away. So I followed him.

When he noticed me trailing behind, he gestured a 'no' whilst waving his hand and said, "No, no, no. You stay here. Get on him and ride. You're racing."

He then turned around and walked casually.

It struck me then.

"Sir, uh Mister… Nathaniel," I called out, jogging to catch up.

"Just hop on, the equipment is right over there," he said, pointing behind me.

And I surely did grab all I needed.

Deep warm breathing was felt on my shoulder, a majestic creature standing like a prince. The horse recoiled backwards. It was beautiful and muscular. A horse. A majestic, mystical horse. I went towards the horse but he went away in fear. Well, this is going to take a while, but it's okay, the same process was done with Copper. Copper. Not wanting dejection to take over, I shook my head fast, hoping the thought would fall off.

I put my hand on his forehead to assure him that he was between safe hands, but he went away in fear. I left my hand, floating up in the air. The realization seemed to hit him, because then he approached me slowly, placing his forehead on my palms.

"Good boy," I spoke softly, not wanting to startle him.

He breathed on my face, hot and fast.

I placed the saddle on him, assuming that he'll get the idea that I am about to ride him. And he did. I hopped on him, and muttered an "Okay" under my breath.

I tried to make acquaintances.

But then suddenly, thunder. Loud and threatening, coming from outside the stable. I looked down at the horse, wondering if it's a good idea to ride in the rain; something on my bucket list. I decided that I will, shutting the case. We began to trot beautifully; it looks like he's warming up. He paused, exhaled a fast, unnoticeable exhale, and that's when I held on tight. We began cantering towards the stable's exit. Then he started to slow down, coming to a halt. And that's when we darted out of the stable, straight ahead into the vast park, covered in grass. The park was surprisingly—or maybe not—empty. I was able to see the silhouette of Baba, isolated in the dark. The moist soil underneath us was crumbs clumping together from our weight. Droplets of rain began to pour on my skin, making it gleam in the dark. It began to gradually shower. The horse slowed down, neighed, on hind legs, and that's when I grinned from ear to ear. He then twisted his head slightly, looked at me, grinned, then commenced bolting through the ginormous dark trees, dodging them all. I shut my eyes tightly. I felt like there was a rock dropping in my stomach from fear. He was moving freely. I didn't realize that we were dissecting ourselves from the park, because as soon as I opened one eye slightly, we were in between the trees. I began to contemplate if it was the right thing to do.

"Uhh," I said, panicking.

The horse stopped, in the midst of the giant trees. The dry leaves under us were grinding under our weight, and the raindrops, drizzling a light shower, were splattering, glittering the trees.

We stood in the middle of the woods, in the middle of the rain. There was a slight wind, but with my wet clothes and hair, I was numb from the piercing cold. I joined pupils with the horse, doubt in my eyes. He just stood there. I gazed at the sky, it was blocked by the extremely tall trees, however I was able to see the moon. I was able to see the intricate detail on it, the shades of gray all around. If I stared for longer, then I would've seen the eerie green aliens that are on the other side. But no, he began lifting his front right hoof, as if revving an engine, neighing, signifying that he was about to set off.

# Chapter 16

## Latifa

Khalifa is nowhere to be found. It's dark and raining, which reached red in the worry-o-meter.

"I saw him go into the woods," Baba informed, worried.

"Don't concern yourself," Sierra's father assured.

But Baba did not seem convinced, I was able to see rage building up inside his chest. He seemed cold yet radiating heat.

"Are you serious? He's my *son*! You don't just set him off on a random horse, assuming it's all right for him to be in the woods at this time," Baba shouted in such a way as confessing a major problem. I mean… it technically is a major problem.

"Baba, it's okay, he's going to be fi—"

"*Really*, Latifa?" Baba objected, unsatisfied with what I've said. He looked at me with hawk eyes, as if he could see through me.

I opened my mouth slightly, to enquire, but I sealed it shut. I knew it was not the right thing to do. My eyes turned glossy, and I tried to blink back my tears, looking down. I was only trying to calm Baba down. I am not okay with Khalifa in the woods with a *'random horse'* as Baba calls it. But I am sure that he knows what he's doing, just like always.

Baba was rubbing his temples, looking frustrated.

Just moments later, the awkward silence was thankfully interrupted when we were able to hear neighing in the distance. And then, out of the woods, came out Khalifa rapidly yet elegantly on a—*wow.* A Magnificent, princely horse.

Relief built up inside me despite the fact that I knew he was fine, wrecking a building of anxiety and fear.

Baba's emotions flipped a page; more like ripped it off, scrunched it, and tossed it in a trash can.

"Alhamdulillah," Baba exhaled. His eyes now tired and needy, gleaming in the evening dimness when he looked at Khalifa.

Baba then had to tell the manager that Khalifa wasn't an intruder, but simply lost.

I ran towards them, with their declaration to stop in return.

Baba followed along, hugging Khalifa notwithstanding the fact that he's soaked.

"Hey," I spoke to the horse as if to a newborn.

I put my right hand out, placing my delicate fingers in between the horses' eyes and nostrils.

"He's beautiful," I said, looking into his eyes.

"I know."

I looked at Khalifa who looked overwhelmed with ecstasy and bliss.

I said, "You're racing," just as Khalifa said, "I'm racing." And we both smiled, but then I asked, "What'd you call him?"

"Still didn't." Khalifa shrugged.

I bit my lips, and squinted up to the sky.

"Hail," I promptly said after a semi-deep thought.

"Hail?" His eyebrows reached the clouds.

"Swift, yet powerful," I quietly said, taking my time with each word.

"Hail, it is," he approved with a nod and a slight smile, and Hail neighed.

# Chapter 17

## Latifa

The day has come. The day in which is the reason we're here. Baba dropped Khalifa off early, and now was our time to show up.

We just arrived at where the race would be held. It's a massive venue with a huge amount of stadium seats. This is big. This day is big. My heart began thumping for Khalifa. We got out of the car, and we began walking towards the entrance. We had a VIP entrance apparently, because we are related to Khalifa who is a racer.

There were two guards guarding the entrance gate.

"Good afternoon," they greeted simultaneously.

"Good afternoon," Baba hit the ball back.

We showed them the VIP slip for proof, and they let us in.

I was walking as if thin ice was under me; slowly, admiring the humongous area and the number of seats. As we were heading up the stairs to find our seats, I paused because I was able to see horses in the distance. I was trying to identify Khalifa and Hail, only when Baba broke in, "Latifa, we better get going before the area gets packed."

Slowly yet gradually, people began showing up, and the race was starting in five minutes.

People who were late were scurrying around, trying to find a seat.

Moments later, all fifteen horses made their way out, going to stand at their designated gates. I was able to recognize Khalifa at number six. I began fidgeting.

# Khalifa

I am standing, confined in my gate, waiting for a signal to take off. I was not expecting all these people to attend. Other than the noise of the crowd, I could hear my nerves throbbing, vibrating my cores.

I stood there, nervous, but I tried not to show it. I didn't want Hail to notice my not-so-confident self.

There were some unclear voices coming out of the speaker, and the crowd began quieting down, eager to view the race, and that's when I knew that we were about to start.

Suddenly, all the gates before us unlocked, and that's when I and the others immediately set off. Hail focused on darting and I began to just focus on what's in front of me. We were all a herd running together, without much of a change. From the corner of my eyes, I could see different shades of white, grey, brown, and black horses, all majestically galloping. I tried to not focus on them, but to focus on the finish line and just the finish line. The crowd was overwhelming, but I thought I'd just not think about it since that's not something I can change. Just seconds of running together, we began parting away, some being left behind, and others getting ahead. And I? I got ahead. My heartbeats began to race; I could feel it. Hail did not slow down. Hail knew what he was doing. He had will power. Gradually, we began dissecting ourselves from the group behind, but we were frictioning against a brown horse. I could hear the rider beside me groaning. Seems like he wants this victory too. I tried to ignore him because he was becoming a distraction; and the only way to do so is to either go forwards… or backward. No, I shook my head slightly yet forcefully, as if the thought would lose its balance and fall off my head. The finish line was getting closer. Hail neighed lightly, and I knew what that meant. I held tight and just then, when Hail made sure I was safely gripped to his back, he went on hind legs, neighing powerfully. Shoot, that just gave Mr. Groaning Man a chance to—but no, Hail landed on four legs, then he galloped smoothly, the sand underneath us convulsing from Hail's hooves. And before I knew it, Hail crossed the finish line, going on hind legs beautifully again. And just then, the brown horse just followed behind me. It took me a while to realize all the cheering. I was struck. I got off Hail and felt a bit dizzy; my sight blackened and I had to pause for a second.

Just then, Hail cuddled me, surrounding his neck around me, and as I began gaining my clear sight back, I heard audible, *awww*'s from the crowd.

He rubbed his cheek on my face and I put my arms around his crest. I felt the love as he shoved my arm away and put his head on my shoulder.

"*NEIGH,*" Hail neighed calmly.

I smiled, pleased, and patted his crest gently.

On our way back home, dawn was approaching. I was sitting on the passenger seat beside Baba, whose eyes were all wrinkled on the sides from all the smiling. Latifa was sitting in the back seat. I looked at her from the rearview mirror, and we smiled.

"Proud of you," Baba said in a soft, low voice. I could tell from his eyes that he was fond, they were glowing like the stars in the dim, night sky.

I put my hand on his upper arm. "Proud of you, too, Baba."

Latifa's voice was thick when she said, "I'm proud of you" – she sniffed – "too."

I turned to face her and her eyes turned from a pond, to lake, to river, to sea.

I didn't know how to act. I inhaled deeply, blinking away my tears of gratitude. My family.

"I am proud of you too, Latifa," I finally spoke, smiling.

We drove across the empty road, silent, hearing nothing but our smiles, the car engine, and the oxygen going in, carbon dioxide out—along with Latifa's final sniffs. The sky was beautiful, viewing an avalanche of red, orange, yellow, pink, and purple.

When we reached the parking lot of our hotel, Papa switched off the engine, now it was silent indeed.

# Chapter 18


## Khalifa


We were back in the park, blanket laid at the same place as last time. I wanted to see Nathaniel, to thank him.

When I got up, ambling in the park, it was empty, showing its vastness clearly. The sun was sending its warm rays, lighting up the grass. It was a bit windy; my hair, cotton candy in the making. When I walked towards the stables, I saw a bunch of kids playing on the playground. They were swinging on swings that creaked, and sliding down the slide. I hated that slide: static electricity.

"Mr. Nathaniel!" I shouted loudly, walking up towards him.

He was feeding one of the horses.

"Khalifa! Congrats!"

"Thank you!"

"You did absolutely immaculately, phenomenal."

I stood still for a second, trying to comprehend and absorb what Mr. Nathaniel just said.

"Mr. Nathaniel, thank y—"

"Just Nathaniel," he interrupted.

I laughed then carried on, "Thank you, sir."

"You cheeky little one."

I shoved the urge to laugh deep down, only exposing a wild smile.

Then, I said, "I just want to know. Hail took me to the woods, then out of it."

"Uh-huh."

"Why was that?"

"Good question." Mr. Nathaniel sounded like a teacher. His expression filled with delight.

"Your Arabian is one of a kind. You did not choose him, he chose you. Your bloods are alike, both Arab. Fight me, but I won't change my mind."

I wrinkled my eyebrows, wondering whether that's true.

Mr. Nathaniel carried on, "He misses the dessert, he used to run freely with his previous owner, and that's exactly what he did when he saw someone familiar, someone Arab. He just ran."

"Then I'm taking him back."

"If that's what you want, then go ahead. He's yours, after all."

"But that's going to be a hard process. Why did he come here in the first place?"

"To race. You were going to bring Copper here too, were you," he spoke, more matter-of-factly, less than a question.

"Yeah." Guilt rushed inside me. I was going to move Copper from one place to the other. I was going to indirectly force him to adapt to a different area.

"Why isn't he back?" I asked, eager to know. "Why isn't he back home?"

"His owner disavowed him. That's what I do—if you didn't know."

"I'm taking him back." I nodded. "And if by any chance you can do too with the rest, then that will be superb."

A tear rolled down Mr. Nathaniel's eye.

"If there were ten of you, the world would be a better place."

# Chapter 19

## Latifa

I woke up the next morning with the maddening blare, ringing sound of my alarm. We're going back home. The room was dull and cold which was abnormal. This morning, the sun did not strike the blinds to gild my sheets like usual. I would usually wake up with the sunlight crossing my room through the window. I got out of bed, all groggy and shabby and pulled the blinds completely open. It was raining. Nothing but the sounds of drops of water hitting the ground. Loud yet soothing. Looking out the window, I could see nothing but droplets racing down on the glass. I predicted a winner and it does indeed end up winning. I was glad.

**************

Before leaving, Baba had to sign a lot of paperwork in order for Hail to come home with us. Khalifa has this plan set up for how he will be having Hail in the desert, and not the stables.

"If he wants me, then he'll stay. If he doesn't, well, he can enjoy the rest of his life with someone he loves. Just because he's an animal, doesn't necessarily mean that he doesn't feel, understand, and love."

"I'm sure he'll stay." That's what I said. And I had no doubt when saying it.

"Inshallah."

# Chapter 20

## Khalifa

I'm in the desert, it's a warm afternoon and Hail is going crazy. Hail was galloping everywhere. The warm wind was blowing, with specks of sand flying around. Hail came up towards me, nudged me, and without a saddle, I hopped on. With the soft brown sand underneath us, Hail went on his hind legs, neighed loudly, and took off, galloping.

Baba and Khalifa were in the car. Hail and I made our way towards them.

"Latifa!" I called out. Latifa put the window down. "Don't you want to learn how to ride?" I approached the car's window.

"No, it's all right. I don't want to take the spotlight from you."

**THE END**

Huda Alkhamis is a driven and accomplished accountant at Saudi Aramco with a passion for volunteering and reading.

She was born and raised in Saudi Arabia. Huda pursued her bachelor's degree in business administration at Oregon State University in the U.S.A.

Her love for books is only rivaled by her dedication to giving back to her community through volunteering. Huda's outstanding mentorship skills have been recognized and rewarded, as she was named the Successful Mentor of 2020 by the College of Business.